Dangerous Grounds
Warrior Princess

Stacey Hunter

Platinum House
Publishing

Print Edition

ISBN-13: 978-1-68096-015-0

Dangerous Grounds
Warrior Princess

To My Faithful Readers

Other Books By Stacey Hunter

Warrior Princess - Slayer's Den
ISBN-13: 978-1-68096-011-2

Warrior Princess - Battle For The Forest
ISBN-13: 978-1-68096-009-9

Warrior Princess - Touch of Death
ISBN-13: 978-1-68096-013-6

Intro
****

Todd Marshall moved through the dense forest, taking a short-cut to the wide river which only few white hunters would have dared. He'd located a game trail that most eyes would have missed--it was just a location where the forest was a little tangled. A huge Tawani black of his safari moved ahead of him chopping the way clear using a bush knife. About twenty five porters trailed along behind. About twelve of them carried a tusk apiece ivory.

CHAPTER ONE

*****

The old lion had Abigale cornered, shaggy and disfigured, his big brown eyes flat and still, he was moving only the tip of his tail; an old disfigured lion but still dangerous. He held both Abigale and Chimp, the pet monkey, at bay in a three-sided niche in the rock.

Chimp stirred whimpered a little, and Abigale, without moving her eyes away from the lion, said, "Quiet Chimp. Do not move, be still."

She spoke calmly, keeping herself stiff.

Abigale, course, did not see this coming. She'd crossed a clearing, on her way to a water hole where she might find antelope for dinner. There had been lions in the tall grass about two hundred yards away, nothing more than the usual and hardly anything to worry Abigale, Queen of the Forest. She'd walked past them. It was late in the evening, and most lions have full stomachs, by late evening especially when they are lying quietly in the sun.

But, the old lion had nothing to eat.

"Run—this way!" she had shouted to Chimp. There was a rocky hillock ahead; maybe twenty feet high.

She could shoot loosed arrows at the lion there and then, but she already knew that the slender shafts would not be certain loosed so fast, and at a target which is moving. Maybe they could reach and climb it in time to leave the beast behind. Or perhaps he would hesitate for a minute, be still, and make an easier target before he entered the niche.

The lion kept coming after her and Chimp, and the minute she was in the niche she knew that there was no time to climb up. She turned quickly and faced the hungry lion.

The fierce lion took a step forward towards her, and Abigale saw that it had an injured leg. She quickly glance at his right forepaw and saw the terrible swelling and the porcupine quills. She realized, then. A lion is not able to resist porcupines; then, with a paw full of quills he is not able to hunt the faster animals. This is the time when he seeks the feebler, two-legged creatures.

Abigale began to make a soft, purring noise and then smile a little. The lion was puzzled, he tilted its head. Very slowly, she deliberately slipped her bow of nahete wood from her shoulder. She then reached across the other shoulder and took an arrow from her quiver.

The shot would have to count. The small arrows had not the shocking power of bullet or a spear and the first one would have to go straight through the heart. If it did not—well, she had only one chance left; she would use, the blue hilted Arab poniard that was attached to her side.

These were her weapons, as well as her quick senses and her forest wisdom. With these the daughter of a white explorer had grown up among natives and animals to become the Queen of the Forest.

Abigale was a familiar sight to many wild things and tribes. They saw her as a tall, slender, bronzed goddess, walking through the lion grass with her head and shoulders very held high, as she sped through the treetops, or making a gold blur against the green forest. Her beautiful leopard-skin clung to her upper body, revealing every voluptuous curve. Light bracelets made of pure gold, earrings and armbands were her ornaments, although she would have been beautiful without them.

Now she put the arrow to the bow. The lion's eyes blinked: in the next minute it would spring.

Abigale immediately drew the bow until the head of the arrow touched the wood. There was a muffled snap. It was not at all the sharp twang of the arrow flying away—the string had broken. The arrow hanged lifelessly in her hand.

Chimp, in fear, cried out: "Chee-chee-chee-chee-chee!"

The old lion sprang.

Abigale jumped, also, twisting herself violently in mid-air. Facing forward, she came down upon the lion's back. She quickly pulled the long knife from her side.

Holding the knife with thumb and forefinger she plunge it in the animal's ribs just behind its left shoulder. She was striking for the heart--if only she could hold on a little longer. The lion clawed and leaped and made chilling screams of rage, but Abigale hooked her knees around its body and held on strongly to its mane with her free hand.

The lion, jumping wildly, slammed into the stone wall of the niche as Abigale had her knife drawn back for another strike. Her hand hit the rock.

The point of the knife was caught for an instant against the granite, and the weapon was knocked from her hand, as the lion came down.

Abigale hung on tighter and grabbed the lion's mane fast with her other hand. She quickly glanced over at the lion and saw that it was bleeding. Perhaps in a few seconds he would fall to his knees. Or perhaps his heart had already been pierced.

Peeking from the corner of her eye she saw that Chimp had clambered to the peak of the kopje and was standing there chattering and jumping up and down. Then she saw the arrows that fell, there in the niche.

"Chimp!" she cried. "The arrows!"

The monkey was happy, he chattered and jumped up and down again.

Abigale pressed her lips together. At times Chimp would comprehend, and at times he would not. And then if he did comprehend, like as not he'd forget what he started out to do before he was halfway there.

"Arrows, Chimp! Arrows!" she shout again. She released her hold long enough to point her finger towards them.

Chimp looked down, then up again. He looked confused.

The old lion tried to bite and claw the two-legged thing on its back. Every time it did that Abigale yanked harder on the old lion's mane in the other direction. Yet she knew she could not keep this up for much longer. The strong king of beasts seem to had more endurance than Abigale, whose smooth, spring steel muscles could possible carry a full-grown man up an ngoji vine and into a treetop.

"Arrows, Chimp!" she called harshly.

Chimp looked frightened and scratched his head, climbed half way down the rock face, then stopped for a second, then looked at the arrows that had fallen from Abigale's quiver during her twisting leap, then looked up at Abigale again.

There was a sudden twang!

As if by magic an arrow appeared in the lion's side, just a few inches from Abigale's own shoulder. The lion whipped around wildly to bite it. His legs became unsteady. He fell.

Her eyes whirled toward the very top of the rock; the arrow had come from that way. She could not see anyone. She scowled. She'd, in this moment, an interesting flash memory of some time ago when her life had been saved by someone by shooting an attacking lion--only that had been with a bullet and not an arrow.

She was facing this lion, charging with full force with just her knife, a rifle had cracked twice, and it'd died in midair. Then a white man had stepped into clear view; he'd called himself Todd Marshall.

He was different. Not like other white men she had known: his hair was black as the wing of a raven, his eyes were grey mist and he had a tall fat frame. He had awakened an odd feeling in her.

Since then she had roamed several forest trails with Todd Marshall, but at the moment the white was in the far Bellville country collecting the tribe's annual bag of ivory tusks back to civilization for them. It seemed he had been gone much too long, and recently Abigale had been questioning herself whether or not she should head in that direction.

Then, suddenly, the lion rolled and fell to its side. Abigale leapt free. The creature shivered, its back legs shuddered a few times and then it was dead.

Chimp, grinning with peeled lips, and chattering for all he was worth, he came running with one of the fallen arrows in his hand to Abigale.

She shook her head sadly, trying hard not to laugh. "I do not need it now, you fool," she said.

She looked quickly at the top of the rock as she remembered the arrow that came out of nowhere. A head came over the edge slowly and into the clear view. It was grinning. It belonged to a black man with enormous cheeks like ebony apples and three or four fat chins. He wore a sub-chief's claw headpiece.

Chimp made funny loud noises when he saw the newcomer.

The man laughed. His laugh was a rich, heavy and deep laugh that came from his enormous depths. The newcomer pointed to the monkey. "The white girl," he said, "has more courage than her little brother!"

There clearly was no meanness in his remark. A joke like this friendly intentions. Abigale grinned back and said, "Chimp isn't fearful. He simply means to protect me from strange-looking creatures that appear!"

The fat man laughed even louder. He glided heavily over the rock's border and with many groans and grunts began let himself down.

Chimp began to copy the groans and grunts.

"Silent, Chimp," said Abigale. Then to the black man, "You speak the language of the Bellville."

He was still grinning when he turned to face her. "It's so. I'm Baellath, sub-chief of the Bellville. And you're Abigale."

She raised her left eyebrow in surprise. "How did you know my name?"

He waved his fingers, which were very fat but still tapered and graceful, and said, "Even the waves of the two far oceans know who Abigale is."

Abigale grinned. "And today you've saved Abigale's life. She owes you a debt."

"There's a way to pay that debt," said Baellath. "In fact, I sought the Queen of the Forest in several kraals before I was sent in this direction."

"Oh?" said Abigale gently, and waited.

His eyes dropped. "There's great trouble among my people, the Bellville." He chanted in his rich, deep voice as he spoke. "What do you know about the Spirit men?"

She believed. She'd heard rumors of the Spirit Men from time to time, although she'd never really met with them. They were a secret group, with members dispersed at strange places, something like the Leopard Society. The Spirit Men were presumed to know all the secrets of magic. "What of the Spirit men?" she inquired.

"They're among us," said Baellath grimly. "The son of our leader, Pokka Na, returned from an extended visit to far places where he learned some of the white man's ways, but also discovered the evil of the Spirit men.

Now he and all the warriors of the society take much homage, especially in ivory. As you know, the lands in Bellville have long since become fruitless of cows or grain, and the tribe dwells solely by its own ivory, the finest of any. Many are weak and many starve among the villages because of the Spirit Men."

"But what can I do to help?" asked Abigale.

Baellath frowned. "I don't have any plans. Yet, Abigale's name is well known to my folks, and they think of you as a white goddess--one of magic, herself. Maybe in some way we can make the magic of Abigale more powerful than that of the Spirit men."

Abigale suddenly had a brilliant idea. "The white hunter, Todd Marshall; has he left the country of the Bellville, yet?"

"Todd was waiting for the ivory to assemble when I left," said Baellath. "There was a small take this year, and he remarked upon it."

Abigale looked up in the high clouds for a moment.

"Abigale thinks," said Baellath.

"Yes." she nodded. "Abigale believes that some magic, perhaps, is the work of spirits. Not that of witch doctors, of Spirit men, but the magic of the forest itself. Most of her life, Abigale has seen strange things. At times one gets a strange feeling in the stomach, and this feeling always warn not to take a certain journey."

"Abigale has that same feeling now?"

"I do not know," she said slowly. "It's very hard to tell." And then she grinned and tossed her blond locks and said, "I'll go with you, Baellath. Together we'll see what we can do about these Spirit Men."

CHAPTER TWO

*****

Todd Marshall moved through the dense forest, taking a short-cut to the wide river which only few white hunters would have dared. He'd located a game trail that most eyes would have missed--it was just a location where the forest was a little tangled.

A huge Tawani black of his safari moved ahead of him chopping the way clear using a bush knife. About twenty five porters trailed along behind. About twelve of them carried a tusk apiece ivory.

The tusks were magnificent and huge, solid and white to the core, such as the well-known Bellville ivory was always known to be.

Around this time each year the Bellville packed and sent a batch of ivory over to the coast, Thorne is the one who see to it that it is delivered safely, and then put the proceeds into the tribal funds.

They were paid half in cash, and half in trade goods, and with these they purchased cows and food and other essentials from their more fortunate neighbors with better land.

The Bellville country was on a long, dry slope that climbed to a mountain range; it was not easy to locate, even harder to traverse and only white hunters like Todd Marshall had seen it. Most of Scott's incredible forest craft, as a matter of fact, had been developed with Abigale on long treks.

Scott looked around him a bit, he wished the Forest Queen were alongside him right now.

It was surprisingly quiet, Scott was thinking. The rustle of the wind in the treetops had ceased; the homing parrots were no longer squawking; it seemed as if even the beetles had stopped buzzing around his shoulders and his head.

Scott slowly glanced at the black men and saw that they were staring about them also.

"Hurry. Move faster!"

Scott called to the men. He wanted to make a certain swampy watering before it gets dark. He was only a few marches from the head Bellville village now, having left early, before the worst heat of the sun that morning. A few hours away from the village he'd entered the forest: it was very hot and wet here under the trees, but at least the direct sun light did not beat down upon his head and shoulders.

The head boy turned around, swept his bush knife at the trees and said, "Juju bikitelo, bwana!"

Scott felt like laughing but he did not. Nor did Scott rebuke the black for saying that magic and spirits were assembling; he had long since learned not to scoff or scold at such feelings. He concurred instead. He said in an identical Congolese dialect: "Aiee, the magic gathers. But if we're quick we may escape it before nightfall."

The others decided to push on, and whispered for a minute or so about it among themselves. The head boy began chopping at the brush again.

Scott kept looking all about him, staying alert—but he did this effortlessly and with little motion so the others would not be worried. He had to acknowledge that he, too, felt something strange in the air. Something more than the heavy quiet—something that wasn't seen or heard, but made the backs of his hands prickle.

Not spirits, of course, but perhaps just as worthy of attention. Scott had walked the bush long enough to know that there are such things as instincts and forewarnings.

The trail thinned out presently. The columns of sunlight came through the mottled forest roof at a sharper slant, and the life of the forest took on the unreal quiet of the late Congo afternoon.

Suddenly, almost without warning, the small safari entered a swampy patch where the trees were less thick and grew from patches of black water. A startled frog, the size of a small dog, leaped from a rotting log with a great splash, and a dark brown water snake slithered out of the way inches from Scott's foot.

He turned. He smiled and held up his hand for the halt. "We have made good speed. Here we rest for the night!"

The porters, grinning back, started to dump their tusks.

A shot and ricochet knifed into the thick silence. A chip of bark flew from the tree just beside Scott at the level of his head.

"Down!" Scott shouted at the porters.

He followed his own advice. He threw himself flat in the next instant, and in the same motion arced the Mauser rifle to his shoulder. He rolled so that it pointed in the direction of the shot. Across the swamp, where the forest came again to its edge, he could see a feather-scarf of gray smoke drifting. He held his sights firmly waiting for something to move.

But instead of seeing anything, he heard something. It was a loud, high- pitched voice and it spoke English with a trace of some accent he couldn't quite place. "Sorry, old man!" it called. "Didn't see you with the beggars at first! May I show myself?"

"Who are you?" Scott called angrily.

"Alec's the name. Ferdinand Alec—just hunting through here." And then a tall, round chested man in bush trousers stepped out from the trees. He held up a hand-made Mannlicher-Schoenauer slantways across his front. He wore a dashing African felt with the top fixed firmly to the crown on one side and his laced cordovan boots were well polished like mirrors even here in the deepest forest. His face was rough-hewn, reddish and pock-marked; he had a grimy mustache and his eyes were a vicious, bright blue. He was around forty years old.

Scott got up. "You should be more careful where you shoot that fancy gun of yours," he said.

Alec, coming forward now, laughed. "Forgive me, my friend. This forest has been getting on my nerves. We haven't seen any game since we left the river."

"We?"

"The Countess Nicholle and myself," said Alec. He tilted his head. "We've a small camp a mile or so from here, where there's a little stream. I should be honored if you would share dinner with us. And your name, sir?"

"Todd Marshall," said Scott. He kept looking at the man who called himself Alec. He had decided that the man was either a hopeless roineck in the bush, or here for something other than hunting. This wasn't game country, at all; a man was lucky to find water buck for his porters in this part of the forest. Scott said, "I can't delay very much. I'm anxious to get down-river before the rains set in."

"I assure you, Mr. Thorne, we won't delay you. We have some boxed India tea that might tempt you. And—"

Suddenly the stranger stopped talking. His fidgety eye had caught sight of the protruding tooth lying on the ground.

"Ivory," said Scott, in a harsh tone.

"Yes, I ought to say it is!" Alec widened his eyes. He moved forward, knelt down and ran his hands over one of the tusks and whistled.

"You seem to know how to spot a good ivory when you see it," said Scott.

Alec stood up and was all smiles again. "Oh, I dabble in collecting things, you know. I've a

surface knowledge of ivory and jewels and that
sort of thing."

Scott smiled. "You know your forest pretty
well, too, I'd say. You can tell those other
people to come out of the bush and stop
covering you, now."

Alec's smile disappeared. His face fell. It was
as though a mask had dropped—for just an
instant there was evil etched deeply in that
expression. Then once more he became affable.
He made a half-bow. "I must congratulate you
on remarkable eyesight, Mr. Thorne. No
offense, of course, just ordinary caution." He
turned back to the spot where he had appeared
and called, "All right, Nicholle."

A woman stepped into the clearing with
three men. This time it was Scott who felt like
whistling. She was about twenty two yards
away, but even at that distance he could see
that she was extraordinarily beautiful.

She was dark; her skin was olive. She had jet
black hair pulled tightly around her head and
fastened in the back. She wore a felt like Alec's,
with a soft veil of mosquito netting hanging
from one side and swept to the opposite
shoulder under her chin. Her loose khakis

could not hide her graceful, almost catlike way of walking and her lithe form.

"Nicholle," said Alec, half-bowing again, "permit me to present Mr. Todd Marshall. Mr. Thorne, this is the Countess Nicholle."

"How do you do, Mr. Thorne." Her voice was deep, hoarse, and she was walking toward him with her hand extended. She wore dark red fingernail polish. It reminded Scott of a leopard's talons stained after a kill. "Please pardon our extreme caution, Mr. Thorne. We fire shots because we saw only your black men, and believed they might be hostile natives." Scott could not tell what kind of accent she had, although her voice had more of an accent than Alec's.

"That's all right," said Scott. "It is one of those things." Scott took her hand, and it was very firm, but ice cold. She smiled at him provocatively as she withdrew it.

Alec said, "You will have supper with us, then?"

"Yes. I will," said Scott. "And thanks." He would have preferred the company of his own men and the forest, but these were, after all, other whites, hundreds of miles from nowhere and it seemed polite to accept.

"Look at the extraordinary ivory Mr. Thorne has acquired, my dear," Alec said to the Countess.

She stepped toward one of the tusks that fell on the ground. She stooped down on one knee and rubbed it with her hand. Scott thought she would purr.

"It is not my ivory," Scott said. "I will be taking it in for the Bellville. They make a yearly delivery of the stuff, and that's the only way they exist."

"The Bellville?" said the Countess. Somehow, her tone struck Scott as a little too innocent.

Scott said, "I'll tell you all about them on the way. We might as well head back to your camp now. It gets dark quickly around these parts."

"Yes, of course," she said, smiling.

Scott turned to his porters and gave them the new directions. They frowned, as they shouldered the heavy tusks again, but as usual didn't question a decision of Bwana Scott's. Behind him Scott heard Alec muttering to his own three blacks, but he didn't pay much attention to that just then. Moments later the whole party was swinging along a second game trail, with the big Tawani hacking the way in front, and Scott was telling Alec and the Countess about the Bellville, and their yearly ivory shipment which they got from some mysterious source.

They hadn't been walking for five minutes when Scott noticed that only two of Alec's natives were present. He frowned. "Where's your other boy?"

"Other boy?" said Alec, innocently.

"There were three when the Countess came into the clearing—"

"Oh, yes, quite. Of course." Alec spoke hastily now. "I sent one ahead to announce our coming. Warn the camp guards, you know."

Scott looked at Alec sharply but the man's face was blank. Scott couldn't quite decide whether he was very clever or very foolish. He

walked through the forest with a kind of
military stride—his shoulders thrown back and
stiffening beard thrust forward—and there was
a proposal of debauched nobility in his manner.
Only it wasn't quite real; it didn't quite ring
true.

Scott had dropped back a little now so that he
paced along beside the Countess Nicholle. She
smiled warmly at him. "I should think, Mr.
Thorne," she said, "Those huge ivory tusks
would be a temptation."

"You mean to steal them from the Bellville?"
He laughed. "Even if I wanted I wouldn't be
able to sell them. The government regulates
that."

"But there are ways to go beyond regulations,
yes?"

"I suppose there are. I haven't made a study
of it. I've spent most of my time in the forest."

"Ah, then perhaps you have seen the
elephants from which these tusks came. They
must be tremendous beasts!"

Scott shook his head. "I doubt if any white man's ever seen them, or ever will. As far as I can gather they're in some sort of a hidden valley that only the Bellville know about."

"Yes, I think I had heard a rumor to that effect," said the Countess. Scott glanced at her and saw that she was looking ahead with a deeply thoughtful expression. She looked at him abruptly. Her dark eyes flicked back and forth, searching his face. She lowered her voice. "It is possible, is it not, that a man such as yourself, who knows much of the forest, could find this hidden valley?"

Scott shrugged. "I might get to it. I don't mean to try, though."

"But with wealth like that you could have everything you wanted in the finest cities of the world. Perhaps you might want to form a — a partnership with someone amusing and pleasing to you. I am not unattractive, am I?"

This time he looked at her in slight surprise.

She laughed at him. "Why be shocked? I may be a countess but I have to live, like anyone else. I prefer to live well if I can. I am not above using any natural charms I may have in order to do it—"

At this point Alec dropped back a little bit, possibly suspicious of the Countess's lowered voice. He grinned at her wolfishly, and then at Scott. "The Countess," he said, "always finds new guests interesting."

She ignored him and strode along with her face perfectly blank.

Scott sniffed campfire smoke in that moment. The trail widened here. Ahead he could see the pyramided sticks and gasoline drums converted to kettles that always marked a safari stop. He noticed vaguely that Alec had moved to his side and was pressing closer.

A sudden chill of instinctive warning went through him. This, too, wasn't quite right, not any of it—

Deafening bullets came unexpectedly from the leaf on both side of the track. It all happened so quickly. There were dispersed blossoms of flame, each throbbing for a moment against the deepening forest gloom, and there were rolls of grey smoke on the other side of the track. Scott saw his porters dropping and catching themselves.

He knew at that very moment that, that Alec was responsible for the ambush. He whirled toward Alec. The big man, at the first sound of the shots, had already jumped at Scott, and now he grasped the Mauser rifle with both hands and attempted to wrest it away. Scott twisted it violently but Alec hung on.

He pulled the fancily dressed hunter off balance, so that they slammed together. Alec was heavy and hard. It was Scott who stumbled backward. He bent his knees suddenly, and Alec sailed over him, but the rifle was wrenched from both of them and fell with a thud to one side.

Scott turned and jumped to his feet, and saw that Alec, behind him, had done the same thing. Both men faced each other, trying to find an opening.

Alec's mask of friendliness was gone and there was an ice cold, focused greed in his expression.

Although both men wore sidearms, there clearly was no time to draw. In the moment before Alec ran, Scott glimpsed the natives who'd fired upon them and were jumping into the trail from the foliage now.

Alec saw they were dressed in singlets and shorts, like askaris, and that each one carried an ammo belt and a low-cost carbine slung over his shoulder. Alec, then, had brought his own small military army into the Bellville country.

The men did not brought along armies with them just to do game shooting. Alec came swinging. His arms were like gigantic cranes sweeping through the midair. Scott sent a hard jab to Alec's midsection and ducked under the very first strike.

There was slabbed muscle there; Alec withstood the strike easily. Scott tried to slip an uppercut at the man's jaw but Alec drew his elbows in and blocked it.

Then one of those crazy swings landed.

It hit Scott on the right side of the head, making flashing lights seem before his eyes; making the forest rock back and forth. Scott was going to rise again, and stumbled, but saw another sledgehammer blow coming his way and just managed to dodge it. Scott slammed his shoulders into Alec's knees then. Alec went down. Scott twisted and clambered to a crouching position and leapt, coming down upon Alec spread-eagled.

Scott braced his knees, straddled Alec, and began to hook and slug, feeling the impact of his own blows in his wrists and knuckles as they landed. Alec began to get glassy- eyed.

Unexpectedly, a very strong and coarse hand pulled at Scott's shoulders. He turned. Several askaris were turning to him now, they had seemingly just finished their slaughter of the porters. Scott tried to tear himself away, he tried to pull from their grips to get on his feet to face them. It was too late. They snatched him from Alec as if he was a rag doll and worried him to an upright position.

Scott wriggled and kicked like a madman. He did actually break free at one point, but very quickly they closed in on him again. A few moments later they had him pinned to the ground. It took five men to hold him there.

Alec loomed over him now. Alec was smiling, but not pleasantly.

Scott looked at him calmly and said, "So you're nothing but an ivory thief, eh, Alec? You will never get away with this, I promise you?"

"But of course I will get away with it, my friend," said Alec, laughing. "No one but us will ever know it happened. You see, it's a kind of insurance. I'm not certain I will find this hidden valley where the huge tusks come from, but at least I can return with this little shipment of yours. It will pay for some of the trouble and expense I've undertaken."

So that was why Alec was in the Bellville country, thought Scott. Somehow he must have heard of the hidden valley, and the giant elephants there, and reasoned correctly that if a man could bring back as few as fifty of those tremendous tusks he would have a sizeable fortune.

And Alec, as the Countess had suggested, probably knew how to market them without running afoul of the authorities. There was only one puzzling question. "How did you know the Bellville had a hidden valley where their ivory came from?" Scott asked.

Alec smiled. "When one knocks around the world as I have done," he said cryptically, "one makes friends."

"And enemies," said Scott, staring at him flatly.

"Perhaps. But I'll not worry about you, Mr. Thorne."

"If you're thinking of killing me," said Scott, "I wouldn't advise it. A lot of people know me in the territory. If I don't show up on schedule with that shipment of ivory a lot of people are going to start looking for me. If I'm found murdered they'll hunt you down wherever you are."

This time Alec laughed hugely. He turned to the Countess and said, "He underestimates me, does he not?" The Countess was frowning thoughtfully. Alec looked at Scott again. He shook his head. "No, my friend," he said, "I'll not be so crude as to shoot you.

That would be messy, no?

What I have in mind is very simple.

I will tie you firmly to one of these large trees with rawhide. You will starve, or perhaps fall prey to some marauding beast. But by the time you are found the rawhide will have rotted away—it doesn't last very long without care in the damp forest. Thus you will simply, be found dead and with no evidence that you were forcibly detained. What do you think of that? Rather clever, is it not?"

Scott didn't answer. Nothing to do now but save his strength, and hope for a break of some kind.

Alec turned abruptly to his askaris and barked a series of harsh orders.

A moment later they had propped Scott against a thick-boled bamboo tree and were winding strips of rawhide firmly about him. Scott said nothing. Not even when the rawhide bit more tightly than necessary here and there did he make a sound.

The Countess stepped up to him, looked at him for a moment, and then shrugged. "I am sorry," she said. "Ferdinand is right, of course. It is necessary we have your ivory in case our other plan fails. Too bad we must leave you like this but that is the way things sometimes happen, eh?"

Scott still didn't answer. Or change his flat expression. But now that he could no longer depend on the Countess having change of heart or mind, he felt that his last slim hope was suddenly gone.

CHAPTER THREE

*****

It was near sundown when Abigale, Chimp and the fat sub-chief, Baellath, entered the main village of the Bellville. The shadows behind the huts and stakes of the stockade were long; the light over everything was reddish and faintly unreal. The Bellville warriors were drawn up in ranks on either side of the central clearing, for the drums had told of Abigale's and Baellath's approach, and the Bellville had made ready to welcome them.

Abigale strode, as always, with her shoulders thrown back and her head held high. There was queenliness in her every step. The warriors she passed sensed this somehow, and held themselves a little straighter.

They were tall warriors, these Bellville; magnificently formed and without the usual scars and tattoo marks to mar their fine bodies. They carried shields fashioned of strips of the famed Bellville ivory; their spears were broad-bladed, glistening and sharp; they wore plumed headdresses that added another foot to their height.

At the end of the clearing another tall native sat in a kind of insolent sprawl on a hassock covered with leopard skin. Even at this distance Abigale could see that his eyes were steady upon her.

They were deep-set coffee-black eyes, and they seemed to lurk in caves cut into a face chiseled out of black granite. This man wore two sidepieces of miniature ivory tusks which started at his headband and curved down along the sides of his cheeks like sharp fangs.

Baellath, only a step behind Abigale, whispered to her. "It is Pokka Na—head of the Spirit Men who waits to greet you. This is bad. Only the Paramount Chief should greet Abigale—"

Abigale nodded, strode forward a little more and then abruptly Pokka Na lifted a hand, palm outward. His voice was shrill but penetrating. And to her surprise he spoke English, clipped, Oxford English that sounded doubly incongruous coming from this barbarously decked savage. "Sorry," he said. "You'll have to stop and kneel. Proper sign of respect, and all that. Quite necessary to maintain my position with these savages."

Abigale took only a moment to raise her eyebrows in surprise, then recovered herself quickly. With subtle contempt she answered in Bellville dialect, rather than English. "Abigale," she said, "asks no one to bow to her. Nor does she bow to anyone."

Now Pokka Na raised his eyebrows. "Dear, dear," he said. "I'd hoped you wouldn't be stubborn, you know. I'm afraid I must insist. And if you refuse—" He glanced toward the warriors lined up on either side.

For an answer Abigale kept walking forward.

"Kaa-ti! Lai-e-te!" Pokka Na barked at the warriors. His command was directed to four exceptionally tall blacks who flanked him.

They jumped toward Abigale. Abigale moved with such speed that she was but a haze. She leapt forward and met the first of the warriors before he was halfway to her. She bent swiftly, she did not give him the chance to raise his spear. Abigale slammed her shoulder blades into his mid-section and then, grasping him by the neck and legs, swung him up on her shoulders. She spun three times, her feet twinkling gracefully as in a pirouette. At the end of the third spin she let the big warrior fly from her shoulders and slam horizontally into the next two, bowling them over.

The fourth warrior stood there, astonished, hesitant. In a half-hearted way he raised a spiked club, as if to throw it.

Abigale pick up the first warrior's fallen spear from the ground. She grabbed it near the blade with her hands slightly apart, took a few running steps and break apart the haft into the ground. Her own momentum carried her up and forward, as in a pole vault. She swung her feet forward as she sailed thus through the air, and her heels, close together, slammed into the fourth warrior's jaw, making a loud crack!

He staggered backward, then fell on his back.

Abigale dropped lightly to her feet, whirled, and raised both of her arms. All of it had taken only several seconds, and the remaining warriors were gaping in surprise. "Hear, Bellville warriors!" she cried. "Abigale comes only to help, and never in anger! A great magic protects Abigale. There is only death and sorrow for any who would harm her!"

The blacks looked at each other nervously and several muttered among themselves. Abigale turned to face Pokka Na again. He was smiling. "Very good, indeed, Abigale. Let us say you have won—this round, at least. I don't choose to make an issue of the matter right now."

"You show wisdom," said Abigale, with just an edge of sarcasm.

Pokka Na turned to the left and clapped his hands. Several blacks went scurrying off to the area behind the huts. "You must be tired from your journey. We will feast. Then you may tell me why you have come to call. Although—" and here he glanced at Baellath —"I daresay I can guess."

Another leopard-skin hassock was brought
for Abigale and she sat there, waiting patiently,
while Chimp hopped to her shoulder and
glared at Pokka Na to whom he'd evidently
taken an instant dislike. A moment later
women and older men began to appear from
behind the huts carrying long handled dipper
cups made of hollowed bamboo trunks. Each of
the warriors was handed one of these—and
Abigale noticed that they drank avidly. They
gulped the stuff, then threw the cups away
haphazardly for the women and old men to
pick up.

Pokka Na saw her watching and smiled.
"Kaffir beer, you know, such as you find at any
kraal. But with a slight difference. I spike the
stuff with millet alcohol. They're forbidden to
go near the little distillery I've set up out there
in the forest. They think I've some magic power
that makes the beer into a drink of courage' as
they call it. Clever, what?"

Abigale met his eyes. "Yes. I suppose it is
clever. And I suppose there's a reason behind
it."

"There might be," admitted Pokka Na cheerfully. "Hardly your affair, though, is it?"

"What happens to the Bellville, or any other tribe, is always Abigale's affair," she said levelly. "Baellath's told me how you've organized a group of Spirit Men within the tribe, and how they exact tribute from the others. I don't like that."

"You are rather meddlesome, aren't you?" said Pokka Na, meeting her stare. "I'd heard of Abigale before I returned—some rather foolish missionaries provided for my education, you know—but frankly I didn't expect this sort of interference."

"Speaking of interference," said Abigale, "where's the paramount chief?"

Pokka Na looked pious. "He met with a most unfortunate accident in the forest. Leopard, we believe."

"You murdered him," she said flatly.

Pokka Na smiled, but didn't answer.

"And who becomes chief now?"

"Nominally, your friend, Baellath," Pokka Na said. "But he can't receive the kaross of his office until the next full moon."

"That will be in a few days."

"Yes. Quite. And, of course, quite a lot can happen in a few days, can't it?"

"I see," said Abigale. One of the women set a steaming bowl of maize pudding before her, but she made no move to touch it. She kept looking at Pokka Na. "Another question. What of the white hunter, Todd Marshall, and the tribe's shipment of ivory? Has there been any word?"

"A messenger will return here and report when he reaches the river," said Pokka Na. Then he smiled just a little mysteriously and said, "If he reaches the river."

It was clear to Abigale by now that much was going on behind the scenes; some of it she could guess, and some of it she could only wonder about. That Pokka Na meant to rule the tribe in one way or another was pretty evident. Apparently, while the paramount chief still

lived, he had been unable to stop the shipment
of ivory that he was to take to the coast. But
Abigale was convinced that Pokka Na had no
intention of letting that ivory reach the coast,
and the tribe derive the benefits of its sale. It
was her guess that Pokka Na meant to get for
himself all the wealth of the tribe, and then
leave the forest and return to civilization with
his new fortune.

While Abigale was thinking of these things
there was a sudden clamor at the gate of the
stockade yards behind her. The warriors all
turned their heads that way and Pokka Na rose.
Abigale turned. Two old men who acted as
gatekeepers were swinging the big portals back,
and as they did so a tall warrior, glistening with
perspiration staggered in. He was panting. He
made his way directly to Pokka Na, knelt,
spread his hands out before him and kept his
head down.

"Speak!" Pokka Na commanded.

"White men approach, O Spirit Chief!" said
the black. He pointed to the northwest. "We
saw them from the Hill of Drums, followed by
porters and askaris, crossing the Yellow Plain."

"They come this way?" Pokka Na was frowning.

The black shook his head. "They move toward the sacred mountains."

Pokka Na swept his eyes over the clearing, his brows still knotted in thought. Finally he looked again at the messenger and said, "Tonight I ask the spirits. They will advice."

Abigale and Baellath at this point traded glances. Something wrong here—normal behavior would have been for Pokka Na to form a war party and investigate the newcomers immediately. Abigale herself glanced momentarily at the open gate and then when she looked at Baellath again she saw that the fat sub-chief had read her mind. He, too, obviously thought an investigation of this white man's safari would be a good idea. Only it was probable that Pokka Na for some reason might not care to have Abigale leave and make such a reconnaissance.

She decided not to wait for Pokka Na's permission.

Just as the messenger was rising to back away respectfully Abigale moved. She sprang from her hassock almost too quickly for the eye to follow—certainly too quickly for the warrior's brains to react. She snatched a spear from one of Pokka Na's personal guards, raced the length of the clearing, her blonde hair streaming out behind her, and Chimp clinging precariously to her neck.

The gatekeepers recovered from their surprise in that moment and started to swing shut the big bamboo portals. Abigale, still running, threw the spear. It passed between the closing gates, frightening the gatekeepers and making them pull away to either side. She heard Pokka Na's harsh voice calling out behind her:

"Close it! Fools, close the gate!"

But it was too late. She had already reached the gate and was passing through the slim aperture. Spears fluttered in the air. The edge of the forest was just head, and only a few steps away a hanging ngoji vine led to the leafy heights of a giant tree.

She sprang, curved gracefully through the air, and grasped the vine. Using her hands alone she sped upward, Chimp still hanging on for dear life, and a moment later disappeared in the thick foliage.

She raced through the treetops then, leaping, swinging, running along the sturdier branches, and a few minutes later the shouting of the Bellville warriors, the Spirit Men, was far behind.

But another sound caught up with her. Before another minute had passed she heard the excited pock-pock-pock-pock-pock of war drums? And then, ahead of her, another sort of drumming, low and rumbling thunder.

She glanced several times through clear spaces in the treetops and saw the boiling cloud ahead, rising high over a patch of forest. It was one of those swift evening thunderstorms that begin just before rainy season. She saw that she would have to pass through it to make her way to the sacred mountains.

Scott raised tired, heavy-lidded eyes and looked up as he felt the first cold drops of the rain on his cheeks.

He could see only dappled spots of the sky through the leafy roof of the forest, but he saw now that these dappled spots were grey. The bright sun light had vanished. It was getting darker. Suddenly lightning flashed, throbbing in a great ghostly sheet for just a moment, then vanishing again. Seconds later the thunder came.

It crashed and rocked like a pandemonium of giant buffalos through the forest. Scott opened his mouth hungrily to the rain. His lips were parched and cracked, and his tongue was swollen. He'd spent a long night, and then a hot, steaming day lashed to the tree here.

Through the night, and during the first couple of hours of the morning he'd managed to stay awake, keeping himself as calm and still as possible preserving his strength. He knew it was hopeless to struggle in his bonds. Hanging on to consciousness, and to life itself, was the only thing he could do.

Before the morning was half gone, however, the grayness and then the blackness had descended. At one part of the day the moving sun had sent a baking shaft of heat down upon his head, making it throb so painfully that he awoke for a while.

But here was water—life-giving water—pouring upon him. His head cleared. New strength surged through him and his vision stopped being fuzzy.

He heard an insane laughing sound to his right. He whirled his head in that direction. Hyenas. The ugly, striped beasts were feeding on the bodies of the porters Alec's ambush had shot down. They would rip and tear at the dead flesh, snarling, quarreling with each other, and gorging themselves as if they would never have another meal in their lives.

Once one of the larger beasts turned his head, curled his bloody lips and bared his fangs for a moment at him. He knew he would be safe as long as the feast there in the forest trail lasted.

He shuddered at the sight of their shoddy manes and ugly, hump-backed bodies. Then he felt a queer, soft movement of the bonds holding him to the tree. Puzzled, he glanced down. The rawhide was beginning to be slippery with the rain that soaked it.

Sudden hope surged through him. The rain would stretch the rawhide—maybe enough for him to work himself free. The bonds seemed somewhat looser already. He strained against them with his whole body, bracing his back and heels against the tree, and they did slip a little— but not quite enough yet to release him. He had to get out of them somehow, now, because if he

stayed here after the thunderstorm went away
the rawhide, drying, would shrink with a steel
grip and crush him to death!

He renewed his efforts. He was weak and
numb, but somehow he made himself press
with a demon's strength on the rawhide
encircling him. He groaned once with the pain
of the effort. He bit his lips and blood ran down
his chin.

Again one of those insane, hysterical barks of
a hyena. Scott looked that way. The big beast
who seemed to be the leader of the pack had
taken several steps toward him and was staring
at him quizzically. His ugly black nostrils were
twitching. The animal's remarkable sense of
smell had detected the fresh blood on his chin.
Watching the beast's eyes, and its very
movements, he could almost read its mind.
Here was something with the hated smell of the
man thing wounded, which didn't move.
Which seemed to be helpless and might be
eaten. But still, the man-smell meant always
that there should be caution.
Scott became suddenly as still as possible.
The hyena moved forward a few steps more,
cocking its head and snuffling softly this time.
Its belly was already distended with food, but

the hyena is one of the few forest beasts who will gorge himself whenever possible, even to the extent of eating himself into a stupor.

Scott tried to breathe so easily that the rise and fall of his chest wouldn't show. This was difficult, with his heart pounding at his ribs. For Scott had a plan: a long chance that might or might not work.

The rain was still falling. Beyond the thickness of the forest it came in a steady downpour, but under the leafy roof it came in scattered streams, where leaves and branches caught it and sent it pouring.

The rawhide was definitely stretching now. Scott could feel the circulation returning to his wrists and ankles, itchiness painfully. Now, as he watched, the hyena's snout came forward and sniped at the rawhide. Scott didn't even dare move his eyes.

Abruptly a faint sound came to his ears. It was muffled, and partially blanketed by the hushed roar of falling rain, but it seemed to come from the treetops somewhere to his left, and it was, he swore, a sound he had heard before. A familiar sound. To most ears it might have been simply a cry of a forest crane.

Certainly it was intended to sound like one. But there was an individual tone to this cry — one that Scott, if he heard rightly, recognized. It was Abigale's call; she used it to summon Chimp without announcing her own presence.

Hu-eeeee — weeeee! He heard it again, louder, nearer, and unmistakably Abigale's.

At this moment the hyena slashed viciously with its fangs. It bit deeply into the rawhide, weakening it. Scott made a sudden effort, straining until his temples throbbed — and the bonds parted. He fell away from the tree. His feet and ankles were numb and he was completely unable to stand.

At Scott's first movement the hyena had been startled, so that it jumped back with the sparse hairs on its humped back prickling. Now it stared at the weak man-thing and laughed outrageously. Saliva dribbled from the corners of its mouth. It took another step forward. Others of the pack, watching their front-runner, trotted slowly over too.

Scott slowly lifted his head. From his dry, cracked lips came the piercing cry of a forest hoist: Hue-eeeee — weeee! The creatures move back again, but only for a minute. Scott listened to the sound of the rain and the thunder which

was now distant —but no answer to Scott's
signal.

The hyenas came forward once more.

"Get! Go on!" Scott shouted at them; this time
they paid no attention. They kept coming.
"Hueeeeee—weeee!" He made the cry again—a
little desperately now.

THE largest of the hyenas was already upon
him. He could feel its fetid breath, hot in his
face. He struggled to rise, but his legs were
without strength, and the needles of blood
returning to circulation were sheer agony. He
knew he wouldn't be able to get away. His
hands, too, were stiff from the tight rawhide
that had held them to his sides for so long, but
now the only thing left to do was to try to use
them. He raised them, to clutch at the hyena's
throat. The other hyenas started to gather
around, snarling and making hysterical,
yapping noises.

A slim, tawny figure came down from the
treetops abruptly. Abigale! Her limbs glistened
with the forest rain and even as she struck the
ground she began to slash about with her Arab
poniard.

The hyenas screamed, and tried to scuttle away. Abigale picked up the largest of them bodily and threw him at the others. Seconds later, the carrion-eaters had disappeared completely, and only then did Abigale turn to Scott.

Abigale did not have the civilized habit of wasting words. She smiled just a little, knelt quickly by Scott's side. She searched Scott's smoky-gray eyes and said, "Tell me what happened?"

Briefly he sketched in his adventures since leaving the Bellville village with the load of ivory and Abigale's eyes roamed about as he talked, seeing the rawhide strands, and the spoor all about, and confirming his report by sight. She nodded when he had finished. She told him then how Baellath had come to her for help, and how they had found Pokka Na in power at the village. "When the safari was reported—and that would be your friends, Alec and the Countess," said Abigale—"he failed to call for a war party. There was something wrong in that."

"Yes." Scott was frowning thoughtfully. Chimp had appeared by this time and was at the moment greeting Scott by nibbling softly at his ear and mussing his hair. Scott chuckled and stroked the monkey. Then he looked at Abigale. "Alec seemed confident he'd find the hidden valley where the big tusks come from. He wouldn't be that sure unless he had some help in the tribe itself."

Abigale nodded. "This was also my thought."

"We can't let him get away with this, Abigale. There are some things in the forest that are best left hidden. If we allow one man to invade, others will follow."

"True." Abigale nodded again.

"Besides," said Scott, "I've got a score to settle with that fellow Alec." The feeling was returning to his limbs now and he was able to rise shakily. The thunderstorm had passed, but darkness was falling. In the very tops of the trees some of the leaves were turning a soft yellow in the light of the fat, waxing moon rising over the forbidden mountains to the east.

"Alec crosses the Yellow Plain now," said Abigale. "I was on my way to look upon his safari, to see what I might learn."

"We will do it together then," said Scott. "Only I'm afraid I'd better eat first—"

Abigale smiled briefly, then rose abruptly and said, "Wait here." Before he could answer she had turned and disappeared as if by magic into the forest. A minute later he heard the sharp twang of her bow. And the minute after that she appeared holding a small antelope by the hind legs.

When Scott had eaten and felt stronger they set out through the forest toward the big plain, using the method they had employed on a hundred forest trails. Abigale led the way by the treetop route, calling from time to time to keep Scott in touch, and Scott pushed through on the ground, taking to the treetops himself only when the underbrush became too thick for passage. The moon was already far above the horizon when they finally emerged upon the sloping plain that led to the jagged mountains.

Here Abigale climbed a high tree and looked all about. There was enough moonlight so that her sharp eyes would detect any moving thing larger than a jackal upon the plain. When she came down again she was wearing a puzzled frown. "Scott," she said, "There is no safari in sight."

"That's strange," he said. "Maybe they've already reached the mountains and found a camp for the night."

"They haven't had time to reach the mountains. If they had struck a camp their fire would be visible."

Scott scratched his head. "Well, they were real enough when they ambushed me and slaughtered my porters."

He was standing next to a large bush which had long-pointed, reddish leaves and from which hung a round, pale yellow fruit. He then stretch to reach one of the bulbs, pulled it, and then slowly brought it to his mouth.

Chimp started to chatter wildly. He jumped on Scott and grabbed the fruit from his hand, then jumped up and down happily on his feet and knuckles.

"Hey! Chimp!" said Scott. "Don't you want me to have desert?"

Abigale bent quickly and took the fruit from the monkey's hand. She looked at it, then up at Scott. She smiled a bit. "You'd better thank Chimp," she said quietly. "He's just saved your life."

"What!"

She handed the fruit to him. "Karatonga. Quite a bit of it grows around here. Witch doctors slice and dry the bulb, then make powder they use to poison their enemies. Chimp, like all monkeys, has an instinct for these things. Long ago, when I could still be lost in the forest, I made a habit of following tribes of monkeys and baboons and eating only what they touched—"

Scott, smiling, turned to Chimp, bowed and said, "My apologies, old boy." Chimp grinned by peeling his lips back over his teeth, hopped up and down again and said, "Chee! Chee! Chee! Chee! Chee!"

"Well," said Scott, turning to Sheens again. "I guess the thing to do is cross this plain now and make a good search for Alec and his slinky girl friend."

Abigale looked thoughtful, shook her head and said, "There's a better way. Baellath knows every inch of this country. He told me that as a boy he even found the way into the hidden valley. This may be where Alec and his safari has disappeared. We'll do best to get Baellath now and then look for these people in the morning."

"Lead the way," said Scott.

Before they were within a mile of the Bellville village Abigale and Scott knew something was wrong—very wrong. They could see the red light flickering upward from the stockade, tinting the sky above it, and they could hear the throbbing of a symphony of drums. The smaller drums made a swift patter, which played against the slower, heavier booming of the signal logs.

"Go slowly and keep to the shadows," Abigale warned Scott.

CHAPTER FOUR

*****

She left his side brusquely and swung into the treetops with Chimp dashing after her. Seconds later she squatted at the bend of a branch in a towering forest giant that was overlooking the fence.

Here the drums were savage and sharp in her ears.

Several enormous fires in the middle of the clearing threw everything into a dancing crimson light. The Bellville warriors were in two shuffling lines, dancing back and forth to the drums.

But tonight, instead of wearing just warrior's clothing, each was fully clad in a rough replica of some animal: there were buffalo horns, leopard heads, elephant tusks, jackal capes--the variations were endless. Pokka Na, a sarcastic grin on his face, sat at the end of the clearing on his hassock.

The warriors were chanting. Abigale caught just enough words to understand that this was a ceremony of the Spirit Men, and that the spirit of the animal he copied was supposed to dwell in each warrior.

As she watched in silence, the drums stopped again and terrified women made haste to go by the main hut to dip the bamboo cups in the vat of kaffir beer. They ran with their libations to the warriors, who gulped, and then continued to dance.

She whispered to Chimp, "He's not exciting them like that without reason."

Chimp didn't understand, but he nodded and grunted just as if he had.

Her eyes darted all around the clearing now, searching for Baellath's bulky form. It wasn't anywhere. And then she saw the two guards standing before the entrance to a small hut on the other side of the village, near the plaintain grove. She could guess the rest. Baellath would oppose Pokka Na in whatever he was up to—

and Pokka Na had taken care of that by imprisoning Baellath, probably on some flimsy excuse.

There was the soft chirping of a tree frog below her and Abigale knew Scott had reached the spot under her tree. She scrambled down again. "Baellath's been imprisoned," she said softly and quickly. "Here's what we'll do." Swiftly she outlined the plan.

It was most strange, that which happened in the village of the Bellville that night. Pokka Na, Chief of the Spirit Men, suspected the cause of it all—but he couldn't very well air his suspicions to the others. That would have shaken their faith in him.

It started when the Leopard Warrior stepped into the clear space between the two shuffling lines to do his solo dance. No sooner was he in the clear, and scarcely had he taken three steps when the unearthly scream of a leopard came from the quiet, dark forest.

The drums stopped; everyone stared in the direction of the cry.

"Play! Do not stop!" Pokka Na roared at the drummers.

They started again; the Leopard Warrior finished and stepped back into line.

The Buffalo warrior came forward. He began to shuffle. This time it was the bellow of a wounded buffalo that sounded, startling them.

Again the drums stopped, and again Pokka Na shouted for them to continue. But by now the warriors were staring fearfully at the forest beyond the stockade.

When the coughing roar of a lion greeted the Lion Warrior's appearance it was just too much for them. And for Pokka Na, too. He was clearly shaken. He stood, pointed to the forest and said, "Hunt the beasts! Hunt them down!" The warriors gripped their spears and poured from the stockade and began to beat the bush noisily. In a high tree, Scott lowered his cupped hands that he had used to make the lion cry, and grinned.

On the other side of the fence there was a swift distortion against the dark forest green and a lean figure holding on very tight to a ngoji vine glided elegantly over the sharp logs and dropped into the village. The two guards at the door of the prison hut barely had time to turn and see Abigale. They opened their eyes in surprise—and she was upon them.

She grabbed the first by the wrist, spun and threw him over her shoulder.

He struck the ground with a hard thud, knocking the breath from him. The other drew his spear back to thrust it. Abigale slipped in under the spear, grabbed it, and twisted it out of the man's grasp. She kept her hold near the blade and swung the weapon. The haft struck him in the temple, knocking him down.

There was no time to undo the rawhide knots that held the door of Baellath's prison. Abigale slashed them with her knife. She kicked the door in and saw the fat sub-chief standing there in the middle of the hut, gaping at her in amazement.

"Come!" said Abigale.

He followed her, still half-confused. The ngoji vine was still hanging floppily at the stockade wall. Abigale managed to help Baellath take his enormous bulk over the wall, grip the vine and swing over to the other side. He tossed it back to her then, and she climbed it quickly, then dropped lightly to his side.

She led the way and a minutes later both of them disappeared into the forest.

The Spirit Warriors, sometime later, returned empty-handed from their hunt, and found the dazed guards and the open prison. Pokka Na was forced to agree that it was probably the work of dark forces, and invisible things of the forest night. But now he had resolved that Abigale, when he caught her, would die. Such an able adversary was much too dangerous to have around.

Baellath lost no time in explaining to Abigale and Scott what had happened, and what he had now learned of Pokka Na's plans. After his rescue, and after the warriors had returned to the stockade the three of them, with Chimp, set out for the sloping plain and the sacred mountains again.

In deference to Baellath they took the route that circled the forest. He puffed along beside them, moving quickly and with surprising grace on his fat little legs, and his endurance never seemed to waver.

"He spoke freely with me, since he was sure I would die," the fat chief told Abigale. "First he claimed that by bringing Abigale I had angered the spirits, and that was the cause of the white man's safari invading the land of the Bellville. Thus, I was imprisoned until there should be a sign of guilt or innocence. Later, he talked to me in the prison hut. Pokka Na cares not for the tribe—he wants only to have white man's riches so that he may return to the white man's civilization and be powerful."

"I suspected as much," said Abigale.

"His plan is to take all of the Bellville's ivory from the hidden valley that he can have carried. I know not exactly in what manner. But he has made a pact with the white man you call Alec, who even now descends into the hidden valley."

Scott understood enough interior dialect to get the meaning of Baellath's words and he said to Abigale, "That might explain how the whole safari disappeared so quickly."

"Pokka Na, himself," continued Baellath, "would be unable to sell the ivory without having the government men ask many questions. Alec has greater wisdom in this matter, therefore he is necessary to the scheme. Pokka Na told Alec the way here and the way into the valley—the way you will also see presently. It is arranged that Pokka Na will lead the Spirit Men in a false attack upon Alec, and allow Alec to escape with whatever ivory he has stolen by then. In this way, none will blame Pokka Na for the white man's raid. That was why Pokka Na made the dancing and the drinking of the magic liquid longer tonight. Thus, Alec will not be attacked too soon. And when the attack does come, the warriors will be both tired and drugged."

Scott glanced at Abigale dryly and said, "A man of Pokka Na's talent ought to do well in civilization."

They pushed on in silence for a while after that. Abigale frowned thoughtfully all the time and Scott, who had been about to speak to her on several occasions, kept silent. He knew from experience that she was planning their next move now.

The walk through the grassy plain which was broken by flat-topped camel thorn and little hillocks here and there, was long and monotonous, and when the moon had reached mid-sky, Abigale suggested that they halt and rest. "There will be many things to do tomorrow," she added cryptically.

THE next morning they marched again, before the sun was high and while the mists were still streaming from the lowlands on their left. They had been moving diagonally across the plains all this time, so that they had been ascending gradually, and were now nearer the jagged mountains that grew like a vast crocodile spine along the land.

They came presently to a low kopje that was crowned by a rock outcropping which resembled an elephant's head with the ears spread.

"This is the entrance to the hidden valley," said Baellath, stopping.

Scott looked around. "Where?"

Baellath smiled, then scrambled with remarkable agility up the side of the kopje until he came to the outcropping. He beckoned to Scott and Abigale. They followed and then saw that a narrow cave entrance was in the rock,

artfully concealed by scrub thorn and a hump
of ground before it.

Baellath led the way. A long, dark
passageway was before them and presently
even Abigale, whose eyes were used to the
forest night, couldn't see their guide ahead. She
followed the sound of Baellath's soft footsteps.
It seemed that they descended as they went
along, but Abigale knew this was an illusion of
most tunnels. After a while a spot of light
showed ahead. They moved on, and the spot
grew and then Abigale saw that it was the other
end of the tunnel.

They came out on a small rock platform
perhaps half the size of a planter's porch.
Abigale stepped to the edge of it, looked down
and then drew in her breath sharply. She was
atop a cliff that dropped away for about a
thousand feet.

She looked around behind her and saw that a
thin ridge of mountains blocked this place from
the sight of anyone outside. She knelt and
stared again into the deep valley. There was
lush foliage below; it covered the floor of the
basin like a thick carpet and the color of it was a
curious bright, poisonous green, not quite like

the dull green of ordinary forest. Mists rose, too, and here and there she caught the reflection of swampy water.

Baellath was examining the ground. He called to Abigale and when she came over to him he pointed silently. The footprint of a heavy boot was clear in the yellow earth. "The white man has passed this way," said Baellath.

Abigale looked around. "But where has he gone?"

Baellath smiled then and waddled quickly to the other side of the platform. He beckoned, they followed and presently saw a sturdy bamboo contraption set in the ground behind a boulder. It was a windlass, fashioned to hold a tremendous coil of vine-rope. The rope led over the edge and Abigale saw that it was knotted at intervals. Baellath said, "It is the only way in or out of the valley. By this we descend, and by this we haul the tusks to the top. The swamp below breeds huge elephants: many die and their bones are found in many places. It is not as necessary to hunt and slay them."

Scott, bending over the edge, looked down and frowned. "I can just barely make out the bottom. Alec and his pals don't seem to be around."

"Exploring the valley, probably," said Abigale. "This would be a good time for us to descend. If we can perhaps block their way out of the valley we may be able to keep them from taking the Bellville ivory." She turned to the chief. "Lead the way, Baellath."

He shook his head then. "It would be best if I return and watch the village. From there I can spy upon Pokka Na, and know what move he is about to make next."

"Very well, then," said Abigale, nodding. "But Scott and I shall return to help before another nightfall. How shall we find you?"

"In the second village toward the place where the sun sets there will be those who know my whereabouts," Baellath said. Suddenly he brought his head up, then cocked it in an attitude of listening.

"Baellath listens?" asked Abigale.

He frowned wrinkling his mighty brows. "It seems that the drums draw near. I cannot be certain." Then he smiled and shrugged again and said, "Go now, my friend. Baellath will greet you again and share meat."

When he had disappeared into the tunnel again, Abigale led the way down the face of the cliff. Scott followed and Chimp chattered along behind. Chimp didn't need the rope all of the way. Several times he swung over and clung to sheer wall itself, chattering and grinning, while Scott stared at him in amazement.

Abigale might have descended a little more swiftly but she held her pace for Scott's benefit. When they were several hundred feet below the edge the rope began to sway perilously with their weight. "Hold tight" said Abigale.

The wind suddenly moaned and whistled along the cliff face and tugged at Abigale as she clung to the knotted rope. But in spite of the wind the air was warmer now. It was heavier, more sluggish, and there was the beginning of a strange, thick smell, a blend of rotting vegetation and stagnant swamp.

And now the mist thickened and they passed through a thin cloud layer, and after a while they were at the level of the treetops. Abigale looked around. The trees were unlike any she had ever known: they didn't grow with solid trunks and sprouting branches, but rather in thick clusters of fronds that spread out as they reached upward. In effect they weren't trees at all, they were giant ferns.

The earth was spongy and moist, so that it gave slightly under Abigale's weight, and about a hundred feet out from the cliff she saw that most of it was covered with swamp water. Here also the forest of great ferns began.

They heard the chunking of a bush-knife and the chatter of askaris and porters some distance off to the left.

"The swamp," said Abigale, pointing.

She led the way down the short talus slope at the foot of the cliff and into the thick growth of curious trees. There were little ridges and islands of soft loam that provided places to walk. The three of them faded into the dim, perfumed miasma of the place, crowded behind one of the trees, whose trunk was covered with crosshatched scales rather than bark. From here they watched silently.

An askari came to the foot of the cliff first; the green-stained bush-knife in his hand showed that he had been hacking the way. He was followed by a line of fearful-eyed porters, each one staggering under a tremendous tusk. It was clear that Alec had found the Bellville cache of dead ivory.

Now the askaris in their sketchy uniforms came along. Even they were carrying tusks. As each tusk-bearer came to the foot of the cliff he dumped his load with obvious relief near a large wicker basket that was attached to the rope from the top.

Alec and the Countess Nicholle were last. They were flushed, smiling: this was a moment of triumph for them. Abigale's eyes narrowed a little when she saw the Countess. With more than passing interest she regarded the woman's lithe walk, her dark, smooth skin and olive eyes, and the way she managed complete poise.

Abigale glanced at Scott and knew from his careful stare that he found the Countess of more than passing interest. Her woman's instinct told her that any man would. Abigale felt, without quite understanding why, an intense desire to be locked in combat with this tigerish woman — to battle by both wit and strength to overcome her.

But she pushed back that feeling and made herself focus on the business at hand.

Alec — his well-polished riding boot gleaming wherever the mud of the swamp hadn't touched them, walked to the stack of ivory, nodded with a twisted whip and hashed commands. The porters lifted two tusks and placed them crosswise in the basket. Alec pointed upward then and called to another two. Immediately they sprang to the rope and began to climb, one after the other.

Abigale whispered to Scott. "He will lift the ivory to the top with the turning handle, then the rest will follow and leave the valley."

Scott said, "Suppose we attack them."

"No attack," whispered Abigale quickly "I've a better plan." Easily and silently she slipped the nahete wood bow from her shoulders and fitted an arrow to it. Then she turned and peered into the greenish swamp behind them. She pointed, "You and Chimp must go further back so they won't find you if they start looking."

"What are you going to do?" Scott asked.

She shook her blonde tresses. "No time to explain now. Move quickly."

Scott shrugged, took Chimp by the hand, and picked his way for another hundred feet or so into the swamp. Looking back before he moved off he saw that Abigale was climbing fast up the tree with the scaly trunk.

A few feet further on, she was out of sight. But there was another tree here in the swamp that seemed easy to climb, a twisted, spiraling growth that was like a giant vine.

Scott mounted this, beckoning Chimp to follow. In the upper branches that bent and swayed under his weight, he found he could see Alec's party and the pile of ivory by the basket elevator, and he could see the tree near the edge of the swamp that Abigale had climbed.

There was a faint movement in the foliage to Scott's right. He turned his head and found himself looking at a reptilian head swaying atop a long, undulating neck. It was bigger than a horse's head. Sharp teeth, like a crocodile's, overlapped the folds of its mouth. Its eyes were small, cold and beady.

Scott's jaw fell. He couldn't quite believe it even as he saw it there in front of him. It was unquestionably a saurian monster that should have been extinct for several million years!

The monster's jaws parted, showing double rows of sharp, jagged teeth and the feverish pink lining of its mouth?

CHAPTER FIVE

*****

Ferdinand Alec straightened his shoulders a bit and smiled very slightly, so that he himself could enjoy the smile without seeming to show the weakness of good humor to his porters and askaris.

He looked at the first two tusks which had been loaded in the basket, and then at the larger pile of tusks beside it. Magnificent tusks. Most of them at least twice as large as the best teeth of even the Tala Forest in Rhodesia. Scattered along the coast, and in the ports of North Africa, there were crooked Greek and Arab dealers who would rub their hands over this contraband.

Alec turned to the Countess. He used his thumb to brush up the ends of his mustache; a gesture that had now become second nature to him. "I've been thinking, my dear," he said, "about this cheap medicine man, Pokka Na."

The Countess smiled. "I suspected as much. I daresay you began wondering how to double-cross him from the first minute he told us about the ivory."

Alec chuckled. "We understand each other." He picked up her hand, patted it, and then frowned a little at the quickness with which she drew it away. His eyes narrowed. The Countess, apparently, was getting tired of him. He had no illusions about her. Given a chance she would double-cross him as quickly as both of them double-crossed everybody else. But on the whole, it was better that way: where there were no foolish expectations from friends, there were also no disappointments.

"Well, then," she said finally, "have you decided what's to be done about Pokka Na?"

"Yes. Rather ingeniously, too, I think you'll admit." He stroked the mustache again. He spread his boots as he stood, posturing. Alec always vibrated with energy, and even charm, and he was well aware of this, and knew how to use it to his advantage.

He kept talking, enjoying the sound of his own voice. "As you know, the original plan was for Pokka Na to join us after we had marched several days away from his country. He's clever enough not to trust us alone with the ivory, of course. He was also clever in organizing the warriors of his tribe into that secret society of Spirit Men, or whatever it is. That gave him enough power and control to keep them from interfering with our little operation here. It also provided him with something of a bodyguard in case we should decide to get rid of him the quick, easy way."

"It sounds to me," said the Countessa, "as if Pokka Na has covered himself admirably. How are you going to get rid of him?"

Alec smiled. "The quick, easy way. Naturally."

"Oh?" She raised thin eyebrows.

"Do you see the cleverness of it?" He brushed imaginary dust from his bush jacket. "Pokka

Na, with his Spirit Men there to protect him, feels secure. His guard is down. The last thing in the world he will expect will be a direct attack on his village by my askaris. Therefore I have the advantage of surprise. We'll move tomorrow morning, while it's still dark, upon their main village—"

She frowned. "You're certain this will work?"

"It will have to," said Alec, laughing. "I've already given the askaris and porters their instructions in the matter."

Abigale, crouching among the bright green fronds of the swamp-tree, heard this conversation. She smiled to herself as she did. She held her bow and a ready arrow; she held the bow lightly, and not yet drawn, and she glanced upward, with Alec, and saw the two tiny doll figures of the porters clinging to the rope high above.

Some of the mist had cleared and the top of the cliff was faintly visible. Abigale's forest-trained eyes could see the porters disappearing over the top. Now they would work the windlass and the elevator basket with its cargo of ivory would begin to rise.

She glanced at the cliff-face appraisingly, re-checking her plan. It was sheer, smooth rock, reddish in color and faintly translucent, like alabaster. There were few breaks or ledges that could be called foot holds. As far as Abigale had been able to tell, the rope was the only way out of the valley—and Baellath had confirmed that. At any rate, her plan depended on this fact.

The rope tightened suddenly and began to move slowly upward, rocking and twisting a little as it went.

"There it goes!" the Countess called to Alec.

The basket swayed heavily, clearing the ground by one foot, then two, then three. It began to rise steadily, as the porters above worked the windlass with a smoother rhythm. The rest of the porters and askaris stared at the rising container silently: in spite of the fact that they had already seen the windlass it still seemed somewhat magical to them to watch the basket move.

Abigale drew her bow. She raised it, tracking the rope carefully. The elevator had picked up speed now: ten, fifteen, twenty feet above the ground. She aimed for a spot in the rope itself, just over the basket. Thirty feet high now.

Abigale's arrow nicked the rope precisely where she had aimed. No sooner had the bow twanged than she had reached across her shoulder, selected another arrow, fitted and drawn it, all in a continuous motion. Twang! The second arrow nicked the rope, too. Twang! Twang! A third and a fourth—

The strands parted, spinning the rope a little. The heavy basket of tusks hung precariously. The four arrows had come so swiftly that only now did Alec and the others react. Alec shouted and ran toward the swinging basket. At that moment the rope broke; the basket came down with a crash. Alec leaped out of the way, and it barely missed him.

The soldier of fortune whirled then, facing the treetops from which the arrows had come. His pistol was drawn. He lifted it furiously and emptied it into the foliage; the shots echoed heavily against the smooth cliff face.

Abigale heard the slugs slap through the leaves and branches all about her, and as she backed away to climb down the other side of the tree she heard Alec call out desperate orders to his askaris.

She was still smiling. Alec and his party couldn't get out of the valley without that rope. It would take hours, or even days for the blacks at the windlass to find another one. But Abigale knew how to get out. And as soon as these people had calmed down a little she would bargain with them.

She reached the soft, loamy ground and turned to move further into the swamp and find Scott. In that moment there was a long, weird screaming noise, something like the rage-cry of a crocodile but twice as loud and ten times as horrible.

Scott, for all his forest-hardness, had been momentarily frozen when he first turned to find the huge reptile staring at him, then opening its jaws. In the next instant, as his powers of reflection came back, he realized that freezing like that had probably saved his life for the moment anyway. The monster closed its jaws again. Its head swayed back and forth, brushing lightly against the foliage. Its blank, pupilless eyes studied Scott.

Minutes passed, and they seemed like hours. Scott was beginning to get stiff from his cramped position in the tree. Still he didn't dare move for movement was the one thing likely to attract the monster, likely to make those jaws open again, come forward and snap.

His fingers, holding to a branch, began to be numb now. Something made them hold on— not muscle certainly, but something that was part will power and part sheer luck. He remembered then that Chimp was in the same tree, somewhere behind him, and he hoped fervently that the monkey wouldn't take it into his head to move, or make a sound and attract the reptile. The only chance now was to keep the thing puzzled like this—if that dim reaction could be called puzzlement.

No sooner had this idea occurred to him than there was a rustling behind him. The monster's head stopped moving again. Its beady eyes cast about; the pits halfway along its snout began to dilate. An oily shudder went down its neck and into the sluggish body below.

"Chee-chee-chee-chee-chee!" came Chimp's voice.

The head snaked forward, barely missing Scott. Scott heard the jaws snap. It was like the sound of an axe striking hard mahogany. Scott moved quickly, throwing himself on the back of the saurian's neck. Here he clung with every ounce of strength in him.

The monster screamed. The scream was terrifying. Scott felt the shrill vibration in the long neck to which he clung.

The huge snake began to flog about in the dense foliage, hitting gigantic branches and bushes flat with its broad, hefty tail. It shrieked again as Scott felt his fingers slipping a little on the smooth, wet neck. He renewed his grip.

Abigale was just coming into sight when she heard this second scream. She had sped toward the sound of the first one, not bothering to go around the swampy patches but clearing them in tremendous leaps and now, as she beheld the thrashing monster with Scott clinging to its neck, she slipped her bow from her shoulder again.

Twang! twang! twang! She loosed three arrows in succession, her movements a blur.

Each sank to its feathers in the monster's body—but they had no effect. It was doubtful that he even felt them.

"Don't let go, Scott! Hang on!" She called that brief bit of encouragement to him. Then she looked up into the trees. "Chimp!"

Two ferns parted and the monkey's head appeared. He looked so desperately bewildered that under other circumstances Abigale might have laughed. She bounded into the tree that held the monkey. "Chimp!" she gestured. "Do what I do. Over there. And there." Chimp seemed to understand.

He chattered, squawked, swung over toward the thrashing monster and then began to yammer loudly to attract its attention. The huge lizard bellowed: a moment later it spotted Chimp. Now, for an instant it seemed to forget the strange creature clinging to its neck. Its head lunged forward. The great jaws snapped, and Chimp danced out of the way. But not entirely out of the way. He stayed in sight—still moving about, still making noise and attracting attention.

Abigale meanwhile, found a hanging creeper. She slashed at it with her poniard, then pulled it to her and working with swift fingers fashioned a slip loop on one end of it.

"Now this way, Chimp. Draw him over this way!" she called.

Chimp took a running start along one of the heavy fronds, then leapt and sailed through the air. The saurian's head swung, tracking him. For just a second it was in the clear, free of the surrounding growth. Abigale swung her loop. It settled over that long neck. She drew it tight and quickly fastened the other end to the tree.

It was as Abigale had suspected. The monster was too small-brained to associate the slender creeper with the new tight feeling on his neck. He pulled the other way and the loop tightened. Then he tried to turn his head to snap at it, and after that he began to lash his tail again; frightened, annoyed.

Scott started to leap from the monster's neck.

"Not yet!" cautioned Abigale. She called to Chimp again: "More, Chimp, more!"

The monkey began to hop up and down and jump through the branches. He kept up his mad chattering. The lizard lunged and snapped at him again. Abigale found another creeper, hacked it and put a loop in it the same way. She waited until the saurian's head was free again, then threw this second loop.

The monster was caught from two directions now. The creepers, similar to the liana of the ordinary forest, were green and strong. It tried to bellow again, thrusting its head high, but that only tightened the nooses. The bellow was cut short.

"Now!" Abigale called to Scott.

Scott leapt, and barely made a nearby tree. He swung himself into it, moved over into another tree and then dropped to the ground again. Abigale and Chimp met him there. She touched his arm for just a moment, and at the same time searched his gray eyes. Just a faint smile on her lips. That was all that was necessary to show her deep affection in this instant.

"We'd better get out of this swamp," Scott said. "Alec and his girlfriend must have heard that reptile scream. They'll be here in a moment—"

"Let us wait for them," said Abigale.

"But—"

Scott was unable to finish. A fusillade of shots broke out a short distance to their left, where the monster, snagged by the looped vines was still thrashing. Looking through the trees, Scott glimpsed the moving bodies of the askaris, and presently the tall form of Alec. The Countess's graceful and slender figure appeared a moment later. Shouts and cries as they killed the reptile.

And then Alec stepped into the small clearing where Scott and Abigale stood. His rifle was leveled. He showed surprise, utter surprise for just an instant. Then he recovered himself.

"It would seem," he said awkwardly, "that this place is full of surprises."

"Yes, so it would seem," said Scott. He had to force the words through tight lips. He could barely keep from rushing Alec and slugging it out—and never mind the fancy rifle Alec held at the ready.

The Countess came up alongside of Alec and the askaris stepped into view, ranging themselves on both flanks. Now, besides Alec's rifle, six carbines were pointed at Scott and Abigale. Scott glanced at Abigale anxiously. Alec's eyes were moving up and down now, as he looked at Abigale. The Countess glanced at him, and didn't miss that. Scott saw the quick cloud cross her brow. Then Alec spoke again. "I suppose you must be Abigale, yes? I've heard of you. I must confess I didn't really believe you existed, but you seem real enough. And—uh— attractive enough, too, I would say. Was it you who cut the lifting rope with your arrows?"

Abigale said, "Yes. Can you guess why?"

"I am at a loss." Alec half-bowed. He had assumed an artificial gallant manner now—an automatic manner that came on whenever he faced a beautiful woman.

"You can put those guns down," Abigale said pointing. "You don't want to shoot us. If you do you'll never get out of this valley."

"And why not, may I ask?" Alec lifted an eyebrow.

"There's no other way out. Baellath has told us that. Your porters are up at the top of the windlass. But they still can't lower the rope enough for anyone down here to reach it. I don't think they'll be able to find more rope to attach to the end. At any rate, you can't afford to take the chance that they will."

Alec's smile faded a little. "But may I point out that you and Thorne are not able to leave the valley, either?"

Abigale shook her head. "We will all be able to leave the valley. But only I know the way to do it. That's why you don't dare shoot."

The Countess, angry-eyed, stepped forward. "She's bluffing!"

"Be quiet, Nicholle," said Alec, with annoyance he couldn't hide. He kept looking at Abigale. "What is this way out of yours?"

"It is simple." Abigale looked down at the monkey at her side. "None of us can climb the cliff wall. But Chimp can. We will gather enough vines to make a long line. Chimp will carry this to the top, fasten it to the big rope, and then we may pull it down again." Her eyes came up. "But there are conditions. First: you must take no Bellville ivory with you. Second: you throw all of your weapons into the deepest water of the swamp."

"What?" spouted Alec.

Abigale shrugged. "It is your choice."

Alec glanced at the Countess but she was looking at Scott. Alec finally turned to Abigale again, spread his hands in a gesture of resignation and said, "We'll do as you say."

It took them the better part of a half hour to gather all the creepers necessary for a second line. Abigale supervised this part of it and Scott went with Alec and several of the askaris to dump the weapons; Scott kept one rifle for himself. Nearly an hour later the neatly-coiled and tightly-knotted line was ready. Abigale tied it about Chimp's waist. Chimp stared at it, puzzled.

She knelt beside him, spoke swiftly and pointed to the top. Then she pointed to the line itself and went through the motions of tying.

"But can he do it? Will he know how to tie a knot?" asked Scott.

Sheens said, "He's done it several times. Let us hope he can remember when he reaches the top."

Alec, frowning, stepped forward and started to say, "Look here—"

Abigale whirled upon him. Her hands moved so swiftly that in the next second she held an arrow across her bow, pointed at Alec. "You're not to come near, any of you, do you understand?"

Alec glowered and stepped back again.

Abigale repeated her instructions to Chimp once more. The monkey glanced upward this time, scratched his head, hopped up and down a bit, and then tugged at the creeper about his middle. Patiently, Abigale told him what he must do a third time. Now, finally, he seemed to understand. He scurried to the foot of the cliff, found a hand-hold, and began to pull himself upward. His fingers found tiny nicks and irregularities in the otherwise sheer rock—a human being would have been unable to support his weight with so little purchase.

After a little experimental fumbling Chimp began to climb away more swiftly and surely. The others stared upward watching him disappear.

CHAPTER SIX

*****

OKKA NA, leader of that tribe's organization of Spirit Men, and prince of the Bellville, stared at a set of blacks who, partly hidden by a boulder from the gloom, were working a big bamboo windlass.

Pokka Na glanced at the trooper standing next to him, he frowned and raised his thick eyebrows to form a question. The trooper, who had a kaross made of zebra-skin hanging over his shoulders shrugged. He had no clue who these men were.

Pokka Na glowered, looked at the blacks again and grin. Alec and the other men were down in the valley, this much he knew, and that these new men were from Ferdinand Alec's safari. They had a previous agreement, of course, that he was not to interfere, with the exception of an attack after Alec return from the river and had obtained the goods. But the arrival of Abigale, and then her escape, had altered the situation.

By now, Pokka Na had thought everything over carefully. It was very clear that he had better examine the matter, and that was his reason for been here. He had only a few fighters with him for security, for if they should stumble upon his shrewd plan in any way he could quickly find a way to free himself of such a small number.

The best thing for him to do at that moment is to follow a path that will not seem suspicious to them. Pokka Na shook his head, and without speaking, pointed to both gatekeepers.

The trooper that wore the zebra kaross nod his head back, whispered softly, something to the man standing behind him, and then he passed the message along to the rest of the warriors.

Moments later the seven men moved quickly with unhurried steps from the mouth of the tunnel and crossed the small ledge. One of the men turned just in time before Pokka Na was upon him. Pokka Na saw the shock on his face, swung a hefty, knobbed club with all his man strength. His temple snapped. The other porter turned around fast. Two of the strong Spirit Men leapt, held him and pinned his arms behind him.

Pokka Na stood over the porter, his devious - black eyes gazed down into the native's white-ringed orbs. The wounded native tried to speak, but there was no word.

"What do you here?" snarled Pokka Na. He spoke the black's language so could understand. The warriors did not understand the language, of course, and so no matter what the black said about Alec, they wouldn't learn how Pokka Na meant to betray his own people.

"The white man sent me here," the wounded black stammered in a feeble voice.

Pokka Na laughed. He would lure this ignorant native: that would be fun. "You help the white man steal the ivory, is it not so?"

"No, no, no. I swear, by the forest spirits!" Lied the native.

Pokka Na grabbed him by the throat. He squeezed the native's throat until his eyes looked ready to pop from their sockets, until his tongue came out of his mouth. Then suddenly he let go. The black gasped for breath. "Now," said Pokka Na, "you will give us the truth. The white came to steal the Bellville's ivory, does he not?"

The terrified black waggled his head, the Congo gesture for "Yes."

"Quietly, the white man would steal as the jackal, and leave before he's seen. Is this not accurate?" The expression on Pokka Na face was ferocious, but he was laughing on the inside.

This time the native said, "No."

"What?" Pokka Na gripped his throat once again. "You'd lie more?"

"I swear. I swear, great chief! The white man will not leave in darkness, he will attack the Bellville village, and--"

"And what? Say it again!" This time Pokka Na was not laughing. His fingers tightened on the throat of the black.

The black attempted to speak, and could not.

Pokka Na let go. "Speak, jackal!"

"Please! Spare my life, Oh great chief, and I'll speak--"

"Well, speak!" roared Pokka Na.

He swallowed his saliva to wet the dryness of his month. "At daybreak, the white man will attack the village. The people and the live stock will be slain. Nothing will be left of it. It will be burned to ashes."

Pokka Na held out his hand and turned to the warrior in the zebra skin. "Your spear." The warrior handed over his spear.

With no change of expression, he turned once more, put the point of the spear to the Black's middle, and he thrust it forward, while the black was still looking at it. The Black fell to the ground, screaming and kicking and holding the wound. He was silenced by the warrior in the zebra skin with a brutal club strike upon his head.

Pokka Na pointed to the edge of the cliff with his spear, and said "Now" "We wait." "Soon, the river-jackals and other whites will appear. We attack when they get here. But you will not move until I give the signal to go."

The other warriors went back into the gloom of the tunnel's mouth immediately, and Pokka went also.

They waited. They kept their eyes on the spot where their enemy would appear, and squatted quietly as black granite. They took soft breath and with such control, that there was no sound of it. Without looking directly at them the eagle passing by would not have seen them.

In spite of the hard, motionless expression of Pokka Na he was churning with excitement inside. He should have known better than to trust a white man with the smart tongue and a deceiving smile, that Alec.

He should have trusted his gut feeling from the beginning, which was to hate and despise all white men.

It was the white man who, sent him to a missionary school close to the coast and had taken him from the forest: his father had not only allowed it, but encouraged them to do it. And the head of the school had taken a liking to Pokka Na. Because he was a brilliant kid, quick with numbers and words.

In his tribe, a boy such as Pokka Na would not be trusted, and sometimes even executed as someone possessed with evil spirits--but to these things the white man took a liking.

There had been a scholarship, and Pokka Na had gone further in school, and then traveled to the cities of the white man, wearing the clothing of the white man.

Well, he was over and done with all that. He would never enter into any scheme of importance with any white man again, although he'd still make an effort to find a way to live in the white man's culture and comfort, which he preferred.

As far as the Bellville ivory was concerned, he would find someone new to disposed of it. In the coast towns there would be Greek adventurers, Syrian merchants, Arab traders, American derelicts; there would be others he could use. But he would be more hands on with his eyes wide open this time, to keep tabs on his partner.

A monkey's head appeared over the lip of the cliff as he watched.

The monkey surprised Pokka Na. It was like a fast sheet of lightning, and when it'd gone, he recalled seeing this creature before--he recalled seeing the lithe, blond forest queen who'd brought it into his kraal. One of his warrior touched him on his arm and nodded at the monkey, and Pokka Na place his thumb on his lip for his men to keep quiet. He would continue to observe for the present.

This Monkey was unusual, it behaved unlike any other he'd ever seen. Its behavior was almost human.

The creature started to haul in a narrow line made of creepers which was attached as Pokka Na stared, Pokka Na saw now, about its midsection. And as soon as it'd enough slack it jumped to the windlass, found the end of the large knotted rope and continued to tie the line to it.

Pokka Na turned. He glanced over his shoulder at his warriors behind him. They all had this dreadful look in their eyes--this was an unusual magic when the furry creature of the treetops could do things such as this.

He took a minute to think explaining that the forest girl must have trained the monkey, but decided against that. They might fear even more a white woman who could accomplish that much with a forest creature.

The monkey vanished over the edge of the cliff as soon as it was finished with its task, and then, a second later the windlass began to turn, paying the knotted climbing rope out.

Pokka Na waited patiently with his warriors. But this time the warriors stirred a little; they looked at Pokka Na, and then at each other, as if awaiting an explanation. Pokka Na felt that saying nothing would be the best thing to do at the moment.

Later, in the village, he would treat the warriors with a ceremony, and dull their brains with spiked kaffir beer. That will keep them from asking too many questions about his relationships with Alec.

Abigale was way beneath them, starting the climb out of the valley as Pokka Na sat there waiting. The rope was fixed, and Abigale had directed that she would climb first, then Alec and the Countess and the natives of his safari, and then Scott last. In this way Alec party would be safeguarded at both ends.

As she sped upward, hand over hand, she felt a strong sense of caution. Alec Wasn't saying much; more than once she'd caught him exchanging glances with the Countess. As for the Countess herself, she'd been much too interested in Scott to return all of Alec's glances. Abigale could see this very easily.

She outdistanced the askaris as well as the two whites and porters climbing behind her; when they were still swinging on the rope way beneath, she had reached the top of the cliff.

She clambered on to the level platform lightly, not anticipating trouble of any kind.

She looked down, saw that everything was going according to plan, and turned toward the tunnel by which they had first reached this area.

There was time for one tickling warning along her back. It came from something beyond the normal senses--forest instinct, maybe-- because she heard or saw nothing untoward.

Only the dark mouth of the tunnel, and the blazing sun beating down on stone and the sand several feet from it. Yet something made her move; something made her spring suddenly to the right.

A heavy-bladed spear came crashing from the tunnel. If Abigale hadn't moved in time it might have speared her through the torso. The spear grazed her shoulder, then glided over the cliff edge and fell away in an extended arc. She felt the piercing bite of pain, but knew it was just a small flesh wound.

As the spear grazed her, Abigale leapt, she was reaching for her bow. She had only three arrows left in her quiver. Twisting slightly, she eased the bow from her shoulder.

Moving backwards a little, suddenly her right foot had nothing below it. To regain her balance she tried to throw herself forward, Away from the edge of the cliff, but her right foot plunged downward and the nauseating feeling of a fall made a sudden, shrill twinge in the pit of her belly.

In that same blurred moment she saw the tall form of Pokka Na emerge from the dark tunnel: She saw his dark, nervous eyes glaring at her from both sides of that aquiline nose, and all of it framed by the tusks along the side of his large head.

Abigale dropped her bow and tried to grab the edge of the cliff as she fell past it. Her fingers slipped a fraction of an inch, then held; she pressed on the edge with all her woman's strength to hold herself there. She quickly moved her legs against the face of the cliff, desperately trying to find a foothold. But there was none. She then pulled herself upward with remarkable strength belied by the supple muscles of shoulders and her arms; she came again to the level of the platform and slid forward over it.

She meant to spring up afterward then, but she never had the chance to. Strong and powerful black arms pulled her to her feet.

It was if every muscle and nerve in the forest goddess body had suddenly burst. She turned, ripped herself from their grips, struck, plunged and kicked her legs out. Abigale hit the zebra with all her strength - on the point of the jaw with her tight fist: the strike was fast and sharp and precise, but yet it sent him reeling backwards.

Immediately she swung her arm the other way, hitting another warrior across the bridge of the nose with her heavy gold bracelet. Lifting a knobbed weapon, the third warrior approached from behind her. She felt his presence. She kicked her leg out behind, caught him in the middle and sent him tumbling over the cliff edge. As he fell, his howl of horror faded—

Pokka Na and his bodyguard was surprised.

They had come to capture a woman and found a wild thing in their midst.

A demoness, whose strength was that of a thousand demons and whose movements could hardly be followed with the eye. There was more than surprise here, there was confusion, also. In a moment or two Abigale might have broken away from them entirely.

But in their very bewilderment at least three of the Spirit men were swinging their weapons aimlessly.

There was a loud snap, loud but dull, such as the sound of a bush-knife cutting into bark. Abigale heard it as a queer, far off explosion and at the exact same time saw a cascade of colored flashes before her eyes.

After that, blackness and the sensation of floating in cold, never-ending space.

SHE heard the drums and the strange, shrill music long before her eyes opened. In this state of semi-consciousness her forest instinct told her to be still.

Moments later the smell of wood-smoke and rotting vegetation came to her nose and she could tell, she was in the main Bellville village. She opened her eyes and waited quickly for them to focus. The first thing she saw were the bamboo stakes all about her: they were driven into the earth, a top was lashed on making some sort of cage. She was lying on the floor of it. She slowly turned her head carefully and then she saw the other cages had been fashioned beside hers? Other prisoners in them? Alec standing at the bars of one, looking scruffy and wild-eyed?

The Countess just a few yards away, and she, oddly enough, still looked unruffled, poised. Scott in the furthest cage.

He was sitting with his arms clasped about his folded knees looking like a pitiful dog who lost its bone. He might have been taking a minute's rest on long safari. His eyes, though, were not missing anything.

Abigale looked toward the clearing. Askaris and Alec's porters were nowhere to be seen, and she could imagine that they'd probably been slain immediately before the whites had been brought here. Out there in the clearing, at any rate, the Spirit men and Pokka Na were assembling for what was clearly a ceremony of some sort.

They were drawn in two lines, flanking the clearing. Other villagers stared in quiet terror-- among the thatched huts away from them, they were mainly children, women and older men who hadn't yet reached the age to go to war.

At the far end of the village a native band was assembling. There were drums of different sizes, xylophones of ironwood and ebony lying flat on the ground, and reed flutes both big and small.

Pokka Na stood in the center. He wore a leopard-skin kaross along with a circlet of claws around his head. He kept his long hawk's nose arrogant and high with his shoulders thrown back.

He turned toward the council's hut and chatted aggressively. A group of women there began to dip cups of hollowed bamboo joints in an enormous vat that stood by the corner of the hut.

This would be the kaffir beer that Pokka Na had made into a drink of bravery for his warriors. Each woman, when she had dipped a cupful, ran into the clearing and passed the portion to a warrior.

The warriors drank it fast, some in one gulp, and when they'd finished they toss the cups aside on the ground. The women then rushed to take the empty cups from the ground.

Abigale rose to her feet. Her head pounded, but she ignore the pain. Alec, in the cage next to her, saw her come to life and his shrill voice, no longer confident and smooth called out to her. "Abigale! You--must say something! You have to get us out of here! I will do anything, pay anything--I Will make you a rich woman—"

The Countess cut him short. "Oh, stop talking and be quiet you fool," she said resignedly. "The least you can do is to die with a bit of courage--now."

Abigale ignored then both. Instead, she called out to Scott in the farthest cage. "Scott, are you all right?"

He grinned back at her. A little shakily--but he grinned. "So far," he said, "if that is any help."

"Where is Chimp?"

"I do not know, Abigale. He got lost in the mix-up. He may--"

The drums cut Scott short. The drums began with a slow, broken beat. The warriors got in a straight line and then began to follow the drumbeat by striking their spear hafts on the ground. They dragged their feet sideways, taking several steps, dipping, reversing direction, all in accord.

The instruments came in. Wailing? Jingling? An interesting, mesmerizing melody curled like

a snake across the line of the drumbeat. The
Spirit men began to chant: "Yo, Yo--Mani
Sokayo. Yo. Yo. Mani Sokayo." Immediately,
Abigale recognized chant, it was the chant of
death.

The villagers, half-hiding themselves among
the huts, continued to stare.

The chanting went on boringly for twenty
five minutes. Then suddenly Pokka Na held up
his hand, stepped into the center of the clearing,
and cried out another string of orders. The
dancers stopped.

Once again, the women ran out with cups of
kaffir beer. Instead of drinking immediately
this time the warriors held their cups firmly.
The drum beat once.

Pokka Na lifted his spear high with one
hand, his shield in the other. "The spirits of the
wild things enter our hearts!" he shouted.

"Yo!" chanted the rest of the warriors, and
drank.

"The strong spirit of the elephant, the
cunning spirit of the leopard, the courageous
spirit of the lion and the swift spirit of the
antelope!"

"Yo!" They drank again.

This was repeated with variations several times. When they'd drained the cups they toss them once again and the women gather them up. Once more the dancing was continued.

Abigale realize that the ceremony was likely to continue for a few more hours. The sun was going down in the west, tinting the yellow haze over the forest red and orange. After the sun had gone they would dance, they would dance way into the night. And one by one they would kill their prisoners—

Two warriors broke unexpectedly from the line and stalked toward the cage that held the Countess Nicholle.

"No!" cried Alec, grabbing the bamboo bars of his cage until his knuckles were white.

The Countess did not speak, she held her head high. She looked straight at the warriors who were now walking towards her; only a slight paleness of her cheeks gave any sign of how she felt. When they opened the cage, she crossed her arms over her chest, ignoring the warriors' firm grips upon her arms she walked out firmly.

Pokka Na gave another command. The warriors lifted their spears and formed a ring about thirty feet in diameter. Darkness was falling and the women rushed to toss wood on the fires in the clearing, so that the reddish reflections danced in the wide spear heads, sending the flames higher.

They moved the Countess toward the center of spears.

She jerked from their grip. She'd been overly serene until this moment, and they were not expecting that. She broke loose from their grip and began to run for the forest. But she did not get very far. Abigale suspected she planned this all along. The Countess ran a few yards away before the first spears came whistling toward her. Three of the spears struck her in her back at the same time; and another pierced her entirely. Before she fell, she ran for several additional stumbling steps.

CHAPTER SEVEN

*****

The Warriors ran to plunge their spears into the dead woman's body over and over again. And when they got tired of doing that, Pokka Na called for more of the filled bamboo cups.

It was while they were drinking the ceremonial draft that Abigale heard from the nearby forest a monkey's chattering. To anyone else it would have sounded like the chattering of any monkey--but to Abigale the voice was as recognizable as her very own. Carefully Abigale's eyes swept over the forest wall where it stopped at the border of the village. Abigale tilted her head and listened.

Now there came from the opposite side of the wall behind her cage a soft whisper to her ears. "Abigale!" The voice was rich and deep --and hearing it she could just about see Baellath's enormous, resonant bilk behind it.

"Baellath!" Abigale called back. "Yes, I hear you." She did not turn toward him, but looked out into the clearing where the warriors had started to dance and where the sound of drums and music kept them from hearing this conversation.

"I heard that Pokka Na had brought captured whites prisoners to the village," whispered Baellath. "I came here, and then Chimp dropped from the trees to greet me. He's with me and trembles with fright."

Abigale said, "Listen very carefully, Baellath. It's not possible for you to go into the stockade. They would see you instantly. But there's one who may enter. Chimp is not big. He can scale the wall and keep to the shadows."

"Aiee," said Baellath, "but the furry one has not the strength to overcome so many spears—"

"Strength will not be needed," said Abigale quickly. "Just something from the forest. You should to be able to find it very fast. When you do, you may instruct Chimp—"

Abigale spoke quickly, outlining her strategy. As she did so the music crescendoed and the drummers increased the fury of their beat. Night had descended fully now: the sky was deeply black and the stars were like hard diamonds crushed in tiny pieces and thrown across it. The village fire flames leapt high, vying with the dancers. White paint and black bodies glistened; spears and shields flashed in counterpoint to the dance.

After a while Abigale was no longer able to tell how long it had been going on. For once, her sense of time was dulled—the hypnotic effect of the music. She saw now that there was madness in the eyes of the Spirit Men, and even Pokka Na, ordinarily strong-minded and cynical, was feeling it. He, at this moment, was dancing more furiously than any of them.

But Abigale's eyes were fastened on a place near the council hut across the clearing. Here stood the huge vat of kaffir beer, and near it the women with the cups who served the warriors. But the women weren't watching the vat—their eyes, like all others in the village, were on the wild dance, gripped by the evil fascination of it.

Abruptly a small, furry figure appeared from the plantain grove beyond the council hut. He looked about cautiously for a moment, then quickly scurried toward the vat. He had something in his hand, and he dropped this into the vat, then ran back and faded into the grove again.

The music and dancing continued and Abigale, every nerve almost to the breaking point, held herself still and waited. The shadows of the warriors were leaping ghosts on the forest foliage beyond. The death chant sounded over and over again: "Yo, yo, mani sokayo? yo, yo, mani sokayo?"

Suddenly, as if by a strange, silent command, the music stopped. The dancers became still. Pokka Na lifted both arms. "We will drink of the magic waters again!" he cried.

The women hurried to dip the bamboo cups.

Abigale's voice, firm and strong, suddenly sounded across the clearing. "Now the vengeance of the forest spirits comes to the Spirit Men!" she called in Bellville dialect.

It startled Pokka Na, then infuriated him. He whirled toward Abigale's cage. He pointed at it.

"Take her!" he roared. "She shall suffer the death of spears next!"

Two warriors had been enough to take the Countess from her cage, but eight of them came forward to bring Abigale. She surprised them by making no struggle. She went with them easily and quietly to the center of the clearing.

Pokka Na raised both arms again in the ceremonial gesture. He kept his eyes on Abigale. "The spirits of the wild things enter our hearts!" he chanted.

The women brought the bamboo cups to the warriors now. Again, each dancer drained his portion in a gulp, and tossed the cup behind him.

Pokka Na did not drink. He kept looking at Abigale. There was triumph in his look, but a slight undercurrent of uncertainty, too, and Abigale didn't miss this.

She raised her own arms suddenly. "Now Abigale's magic begins!"

It was timed perfectly. No sooner had she spoken than strange things began to happen. One of the Spirit Men suddenly clapped his hands to his stomach and groaned. Others stared about stupidly, puzzled, bewildered. A warrior in a lion's mane cried suddenly, "Water!" He began to run toward the council hut, then abruptly stumbled and fell.

Some of the warriors now began to make choking sounds. Others were grabbing desperately at aching throats. One raced, screaming for the plantain grove, fell and then began to kick himself in a flat, spasmodic circle on the ground.

Before another minute had passed not a warrior was still standing.

Except Pokka Na. His initial surprise had gone. He was staring at Abigale now, beginning to suspect a little of what must have happened. But Abigale had the advantage of surprise in this moment, and she meant to keep it. Coolly, right before Pokka Na's eyes, she picked up a bush-knife that one of the fallen warriors had dropped. She walked over to Scott's cage.

Scott grinned at her through the bamboo bars and said, "I knew all the time you'd do it."

She smiled fleetingly, chopped the rawhide cage fastenings apart, and Scott stepped into the open.

"Abigale! You cannot forget me! You must release me, too, Abigale!" screamed Alec.

Abigale looked at him in disgust—but nevertheless walked over to his cage and cut the thongs.

Pokka Na suddenly roared a terrible sound of anger and frustration. He raised his spear and narrowed his eyes at Abigale. She whirled toward him. There was no time to rush him with her bush-knife, nor was there time to scoop a fallen spear from the ground.

"Look out, Abigale!" Scott cried. It distracted Pokka Na for a moment. He turned his eyes toward Scott and in doing that he saw Alec again. He saw him as if for the first time.

His brow clouded even more, as if with a new gust in a rainstorm already raging. His close-set eyes glittered in their deep sockets: this was the man who had brought all of it about; here was the man who had tried to make a fool of him.

Pokka Na's spear arm racked back.

Alec had just enough time to widen his eyes and cry, "No!"

The spear came forward in a slight, almost imperceptible curve, streaking across the distance between the two men. Alec tried to dodge. The heavy point caught him, with a sound like a knife striking a rotten apple, in the left breast.

The force of the thing slammed him against the cage he had just left. He leaned there for a moment looking stupidly down at the weapon in his body. Then he sank slowly, his eyes still open, and a second later he was sitting there, dead.

Abigale lost no time as all of this happened. She pounced on another fallen spear, then faced Pokka Na, holding the weapon lightly and ready to throw.

He turned and stared at her, His eyes were filmed over; in them was the hopelessness of a man who has lost everything. Yet he was not afraid; he squared his shoulders and stuck his chest forward, waiting for Abigale to strike.

There was a sudden clamor at the stockade gate and women ran to open it. As they watched, Baellath entered. The big native was dressed in the ceremonial costume of a full chief of the Bellville. He walked slowly across the compound with his curious fat man's grace. He held a spear, too. He stopped twenty paces from Pokka Na and kept his eyes on the usurper. Then he glanced at Abigale for a brief instant. "Give him a spear, too, O Abigale."

Abigale understood. By the code of the tribe it was necessary for Baellath to kill Pokka Na with his own hand—and by choice Baellath was offering him an equal combat. The Bellville would long remember how their rightful chief acted in this matter.

"Do as he says. Pick up a spear," she said to Pokka Na.

He moved slowly, and with his eyes still on Baellath. Holding their weapons then, the two men faced each other—one long, sinewy and nervous; the other fat, but tapered and graceful.

"Hai!" said Abigale abruptly, giving the signal.

Pokka Na hurled his spear desperately and with an arcing motion of his long body. Baellath barely seemed to move. The tall black's spear hurtled by Baellath, just missing his shoulder—and Baellath's spear struck the leader of the Spirit Men in the very center of his torso?

It was three days later. Three people stood at the edge of a great forest.

"And now the trail parts," said Abigale.

Baellath nodded, and pointed northwest: "In this direction Scott takes the Bellville ivory—" and southwest: "while Abigale returns to her own forest. Abigale departs and takes her magic with her."

Abigale laughed. "Abigale's magic is only that of the forest. For only the forest has magic. The forest knew from the first that the white man, Alec, came to steal from it, and thus he was doomed. Pokka Na, who went against the way of the forest, was also marked for death. The forest has all it needs to perform its magic—such as the poisonous karatonga which you were able to find, and which Chimp was able to drop in the vat of kaffir beer."

Platinum House
Publishing

By Stacey Hunter
Touch of Death

Hunger stalked the land. Rain had forsaken the village.
And the voracious Abama Warriors led by Abigale—
Goddess of all the Forest. The Golden Goddess—
paraded persistently against the walls of the Great
Kilmer to lay to rest the prehistoric curse of Leman bin
Ali.

******

Abigale shook water from her long golden locks and
stepped out of the swimming pool, majestic, her
tanned beauty glowing bright in the sunlight.

The hot sun hugged her slender frame and quickly
swallowed the moisture from her body. She then
rushed across to the hut which stood on two poles, six
feet over the ground. She got dress into leopard skin
clothing and walked towards the doorway of the little
hut, looking out across the swimming pool.

Print Edition
ISBN-13: 978-1-68096-013-6

Platinum House
Publishing

By Stacey Hunter
Battle For The Forest

******

Abigale lay still on the bed of green grasses, her hands clutched behind her beautiful blond head. She was touched by a gentle wind blowing from the south through the wide open door of the tree house, whispered of a forest long awake and very busy.

But this morning the noises from the forest held no interest for Abigale. A feeling of loneliness and sadness had gripped her from the moment she woke up.

In nearby tree tops her pet monkey, Chimp, had left his noisy pursuits since sunrise to peer anxiously in the doorway in a mistress who'd lie on such a day that was so wonderful.

Print Edition
ISBN-13: 978-1-68096-009-9

Platinum House
Publishing

By Stacey Hunter
Slayer's Den

Violent and unwavering was the Forest's allegiance to
the wing-footed goddess—all but Galagi Yamo, famous
shaker of the earth, the ancient Kalundas, who
surrender to no law but his insidious juju.

******

Abigale quickly dropped from the branches of an
enormous, spreading baobab and started to climb the
rocky krantz, jumping lightly from rock to rock.

She was so skilled and well balanced that her slender
body seemed to move, without particularized motion;
and she flow with incredible swiftness in whatever
direction her energy suggested, her beautiful bronzed
limbs flashing in the sunlight, her golden hair flowing
behind.
On the top of the hill Abigale unslung her bow and
quiver, looking about for somewhere to rest. She
picked a place where a mimosa grew out of a grassy
cleft and, with feline elegance stretched out flat on her
stomach in the black pool of its shadow.

Print Edition
ISBN-13: 978-1-68096-011-2

Dangerous Grounds